This Book Belongs To

Text copyright 2022 by CharLene Seay. Illustrations copyright 2022 by Jennifer Tipton Cappoen. All rights reserved. No part of this book may be reproduced or transmitted in any form or by any means, electronic or mechanical, including photography, recording, or any information storage and retrieval system, without permission in writing from the publisher. The only exceptions are brief excerpts and reviews.

Author: CharLene Seay
Cover Designer and Illustrator: Jennifer Tipton Cappoen
Editorial Assistant: Connie S. Graham
Editor: Lynn Bemer Coble

PCKids is an imprint of **Paws and Claws Publishing, LLC.**
1589 Skeet Club Road, Suite 102 #175
High Point, NC 27265
www.PawsandClawsPublishing.com
info@pawsandclawspublishing.com

ISBN # 978-1-946198-31-0
Printed in the United States

SAM AND FLAM
FOREVER FRIENDS

by
CharLene Seay

Illustrated by Jennifer Tipton Cappoen

Acknowledgement

Connie S. Graham is Charlene's daughter. She's a retired elementary-school principal, so she understands well how important books and the love of reading are for children.

Connie has been CharLene's right-hand person throughout the writing and editing of this book. Without Connie's help and support the entire time, CharLene never could have written and completely edited her hermit-crab book. Connie typed all the text for the book, helped rewrite the text, made lots of suggestions, and listened to her mother and to her editor with whom they worked in editing sessions on the phone. As Editorial Assistant, Connie encouraged CharLene in many ways, motivated her to continue working on the book when she didn't think she could do so any longer, and was always there for her mother.

CharLene's daughter is a meticulous organizer who keeps everyone around her organized. That's the quintessential definition of a good elementary-school principal too.

Thank you for all you've done to help make my book a reality, Connie.
Momma

Dedications

In loving memory of my mother Emma Miller; my youngest daughter Sherry Seay; my husband Col. John Lewis Patrick, Jr.; my only brother Leroy Miller; and my baby sister Brenda Craidon.

My mother, Emma Miller, gave me life, love, and support. She was with me a lot of my entertainment years.

She had Alzheimer's, but she never forgot my name or whom I was. She spoke about "her CharLene" to staff members at the nursing home all the time. During my first visit to see Mother at the rest home, when the staff members heard my name, they approached me and asked, "Are you the CharLene Emma is always talking about?"

To my beautiful and oh-so-talented daughter, Sherry Seay. Sherry always encouraged me and supported my efforts in anything I pursued. She would be so proud and excited to know I wrote and published a children's book.

My Prandsome Hince, as I labeled him. My husband was better known as Col. John Lewis Patrick, Jr. He loved his "Cinderella," as he always called me.

He was so passionate about my singing, my piano playing, and my entertainment career. He encouraged me to continue both entertaining and writing and to pursue this children's book. He loved it!

We had a fairy-tale initial meeting and marriage.

My only brother, Leroy Miller, took pride in all my talents and in being my brother.

He sang in gospel quartets. His was the deepest voice, and everyone got excited about it.

He was as strong as they come. Due to his talents, he was known as the best brick mason in Eastern Tennessee.

He was such a pool shark that at his funeral, they arranged all the pool balls as candles in a rack.

My baby sister, Brenda Craidon, was a first-grade teacher for more than 30 years. She loved children and loved to read all genres of children's books.

She was my confidante and my running buddy. We were two peas in a pod!

My sister would've been so very proud of the book I'd written.

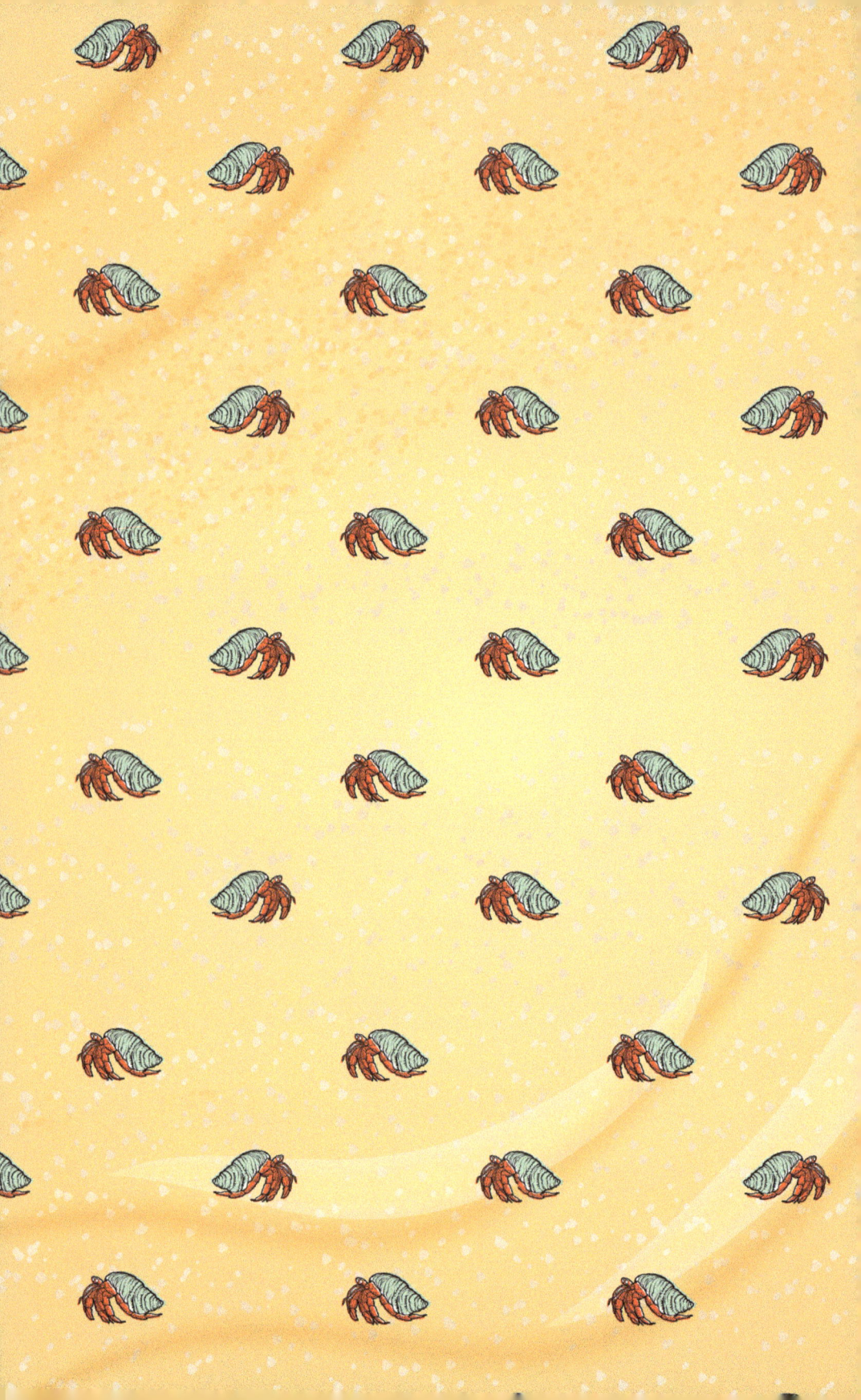

TABLE OF CONTENTS

The Bucket Man 11

Sam and Flam 17

If We Were Fish, … 21

Feels Like the Beach Again 29

The Neighbor Kids Meet Sam and Flam 37

Two New Friends and a Shell 45

Little John 49

Forever Friends 53

Gratitude 57

About the Author 59

As I relate to you this adventure-filled story of Sam and Flam,
    I want you to know
That I've had many hermit crabs to love over the years, so this
    story must be told.

Before the friends met each other, lots of things took place.
You'll love all their adventures. Hear what I say.

Here's some information so you'll better understand.
This tells you many things about hermit crabs and how they
    live on land.

Even though each hermit crab is born in the ocean,
    one day it might come onto the shore.
If it does, it will need to find a shell for a home. Or its life
    will be no more.

It's strange to see a hermit crab naked as it searches for
    a shell.
It looks like an unshelled peanut with legs. It's fragile.
    You can tell.

When the hermit crab comes upon a snail or another such
    creature moving along the beach,
The snail knows what's ahead for it, so it gives up its needs.

The crab takes the snail's shell. Then it moves the snail out
    of the way.
After making that change, the hermit crab feels safe in its new
    shell as it grows more every day.

As time goes by, again the crab grows so big that it will
    need a still larger shell.
Soon the hermit crab will find the shell it wants and check
    it over well.

If another hermit crab lives inside the chosen shell, the two crabs might end up in a fight.
Behold, it sees a crab inside the shell and watches it move. It's time for a fight or flight.

The crab outside the shell will attempt to prove who's who as it raises its claws into the air and then jerks well.
With its large claw, it tries its best to pull the crab out of the shell.

Sometimes the crab won't come out even after it loses a body part, which eventually will replace itself when the crab molts.
Other times the crab inside will stay until death, while at other times it bolts.

Finally the crab in the shell gives up. The other crab won. It was worth the battle.
The lucky aggressor has an empty shell to slide its body into.

The crab slides its stomach in first as fast as lightning. Wow, what a perfect fit.
It's safe now, can walk away, and will continue to grow bigger every day, bit by bit.

The crab that was in the shell and lost the fight will have to find a new home.
Starting on its shell-finding journey, it will begin to roam.

With their four pairs of legs used for walking and their large, purple claws, hermit crabs really *move*. Sometimes they'll even fall.
They climb onto the backs of other hermit crabs, like climbing up a wall.

THE BUCKET MAN

Well, the ocean currents pushed two large hermit crabs onto the shore.
It wasn't long before Bob the Bucket Man came along wearing his trademark sun hat. He scooped the crabs up like sweeping dust off the floor.

After doing that, he began whistling and walking. Bob walked as fast as he could.
He wanted to arrive at the Superstore soon. It wasn't long until that came true. There he was. There he stood!

He took a moment and breathed a deep breath. He heard the door slam behind him as he walked right in.
At the same time, some clerks inside announced, "Bob the Bucket Man is here," as all of them grinned.

The clerks ran over to him voicing, "Hurry, Bob. Show us what you have in your bucket! We're anxious to see what you've brought us."
Bob lifted the bucket onto the counter. When the clerks looked inside, they blurted out, "Oh my gosh, oh my gosh," as they chuckled.

The head clerk spoke, "Bob, how did you get these? They're the biggest hermit crabs I've ever seen."
Bob shrugged his shoulders, snickered, and uttered, "Beats me. I was just searching the beach.

Suddenly out of the blue, I spotted a large hermit crab move.
That wasn't all. As I looked out of the corner of my eye, I saw that there were two.

They were crawling right at the water's edge. That left me stunned.
Since the tide was coming in so rapidly, there was no time to waste. I'd have to hurry and run.

Run I did! I moved as fast as my shaky legs would go.
I realized that crabs are second only to the snake for disappearing. I couldn't lose those crabs, don't you know?

It freaked me out a little to have to get there so quickly, but I couldn't quit.
Oh, how exciting it was to scoop them into my bucket when I did.

Once I had them in my possession, it made my heart content.
With that wild, tricky encounter ending, I had to get a grip.

After all that commotion, I felt proud. I smiled, knowing that the large crabs take more effort to find. Then I moved like lightning to get here.
How could I keep myself from hollering, 'Whoopee;' throwing my hat into the air; and letting out a big cheer?"

The clerks shrieked with laughter over what Bob told them about his unusual experience.
Once they settled down, the head clerk declared, "C'mon, Bob. Let's go to the back where the crab cage sits. It's time to get serious."

As they walked, the clerk stated, "You know, Bob, our hermit crabs are given the best of care.
We appreciate the crabs that you bring us. They're the happiest crabs in any store anywhere."

As they arrived at the cage, some customers had gathered to ask questions about the crabs inside.
The cage was completely covered with wire, stood on stilts, and was big and wide.

Bob said hi to everyone as he reached into his bucket.
Then he set the large crabs in the cage. That made the other crabs look like little nuggets.

Immediately the customers lit up with delight
As they watched the other crabs move away quickly as if they were on fire. It was an astonishing sight!

Bob had taken good care of the large crabs and felt good as he got ready to leave.
He felt lucky to have found such big crabs. It was almost hard to believe!

As Bob turned to the clerk to say good-bye, he closed the cage lid. That's when the crabs heard the click of the lock.
The hermit crabs were so alarmed at the sound that they nearly jumped out of their skin. Whoops, I mean shells! Boy, oh boy, need I say those crabs were in shock.

After some time, the crabs no longer felt uptight, and they began looking around. They saw lots of folks close by browsing in the store and saw novelties sitting on the shelves.
The hermit crabs sat over in a corner where a sign beside their big cage read *Hermit Crabs for Sale.*

Their eyes are bright and look like eyeballs sitting on stilts.
Crabs can look in every direction according to their wills.

As Bob walked to the front of the store to leave, the crowd near the crab cage was getting louder with anticipation.
They watched some smaller crabs ride piggyback on the two larger crabs. What an attraction!

The Bucket Man laughed, tipped his hat to say good-bye, and went on his way.
He was pleased to hear the interaction the customers had as the crabs entertained them. Bob told the clerks farewell and said happily, "I'll bring you more crabs another day."

The two large hermit crabs questioned, "Is this where we will *stay?*"
They didn't know what to think about this strange, enormous place.

SAM AND FLAM

In the crabs' cage in this new place, all those hermit crabs moved *everywhere.*
Everything around them was strange, so the two newest crabs just sat there.

The ocean's currents had changed their lives forever by pulling the poor hermit crabs from their mothers.
In the ocean, they'd never had a problem. Never. Never. Not ever!

What was happening meant that the two of them *didn't* move, because they didn't have a clue what to do.
They were still very scared and knew they needed a minute or two.

They sat and thought. Then one of them spoke up
and asked,
"Do you know what's going on or how long this is going
to last?

I'm feeling all alone. Why couldn't we be friends?"
"Yes. Why not?" the other one replied. "Just tell
me when."

As they stared directly at each other, they realized that
they looked exactly the same!
One hermit crab pointed out the obvious question,
"Won't we need names?"

The other chimed in, "That's a good idea. Let's think
a bit."
As they were thinking as hard as they could, one spoke up
and exclaimed, "Oh, I've got it. I've got it!

How about Sam and Flam? Those two names rhyme
and blend.
That will make us happy, and folks will think we're kin."

The two hermit crabs agreed. Sam and Flam would be
their names. Then their uncertainty would come
to an end.
Sam and Flam tapped their claws together and
announced, *"We're forever friends!"*

IF WE WERE FISH,...

You see, Sam and Flam were hermit crabs. And they were
   big crabs too.
They looked quite ugly and scary. You'd think they weren't
   cute.

Well, at the beach in the Superstore where many tourists
   came through,
Not one soul would buy them. The visitors simply mouthed,
   "Ooooooooooooooh!"

Every time that happened, it hurt Sam and Flam's feelings,
   because they longed for a home.
Since they were bored by where they lived, the forever
   friends were always ready to roam.

Sam and Flam were very sad. Then much to their surprise,
They heard a woman at their cage request, "I want two hermit crabs to buy."

The woman chose Sam and Flam and forgot all the rest.
She articulated, "Please put them in a box for me. That will be the best."

The hermit crabs were placed into a box. *O-o-o-o-o-o-h, it was really dark.*
Poor Sam and Flam were sliding everywhere. They couldn't get a grip. *Oh my, what a start.*

The woman set her box of crabs into the cart.
She felt satisfied about buying two crabs instead of one. Crabs get lonely, so that was smart.

Even though they are called hermit crabs, they're not hermits at all.
They love to socialize in groups that are big, medium, and small.

In the wild, you might find crabs together with up to 100 or more.
Then you realize all the fun they have since they're never bored.

The woman continued to shop, looking for the recommended crab food.
There were other foods she needed to purchase, so the next day she'd buy them at the market. Crabs really love and need fresh proteins, vegetables, and fruits.

Crabs become stressed out easily, so Sam and Flam were becoming fatigued. Since Flam was mad and ready to complain, he asked,
"Why is this taking so long? We'd rather be using our time having fun in sand somewhere digging."

Surprisingly the woman was exiting at the door of the store. After getting outdoors, she noticed that it looked as if rain were coming.
Out of the clear, someone close by was rapidly walking.

It was Stephen and Shannon, a young neighborhood couple she knew.
Therefore, it was natural for her to call out to them, "Hey, you two."

They stopped, turned, and realized it was Emma. *What a nice surprise* they thought. They approached her with greetings and a hug.
Stephen stated, "I can see you've been shopping." "Yes," Emma laughingly responded, "I just bought two hermit crabs to enjoy and love."

Stephen requested, "Well, let us see your crabs." Emma was delighted to open the box the crabs were in. Her face beamed.
When Stephen and Shannon looked at the crabs, they stepped back in amazement and said in unison, "Wow! They're the biggest crabs we've ever seen!"

The three of them began to laugh at their reaction to Emma's enormous crabs. Inside the box, Sam and Flam wondered, *What is so funny? Why are they laughing so hard and loud?*
Stephen said, "Emma, I feel sprinkles. We'd better get you to your car by the look of those rain clouds."

Emma agreed, "Okay, let's go. I'm anxious to see my crab pets inside the 60-gallon glass tank where I've created a habitat for them that might feel natural.
They'll love that much space in order to burrow completely. Hopefully the six inches of sand substrate mixture I added and leveled in the floor of the tank will make everything feel familiar. If it does, that will be special."

In haste Stephen began directing Emma and Shannon to the car. He hoped that they could beat the rain.
"Get your keys out, Emma, so we'll have no problem leaving quickly. That will be our aim."

Stephen pushed the cart to where Emma was parked and lifted her purchases out easily.
Then he handed Shannon the box of crabs for the backseat and suggested, "Make sure you place them safely."

Stephen carried Emma's other purchases to the front seat and set them down beside her. He told Emma to start the car because Shannon had finished in the back.
As the car started, Shannon heard commotion from the crabs. It sounded as if they were being attacked.

Shannon peeked into their box and explained to the crabs, "You're going to be so happy where you'll be living. The ride over there is not very far.
Be looking out for me in your new home, because I'll be bringing you treats such as seaweed, nuts, and fish flakes. You're surely hermit-crab superstars."

Emma was ready to go and offered to drive the couple home. Stephen thanked her and said, "I think we'll be all right because it looks as if the rain has passed at last."
They all gave a sigh of relief, said their good-byes, and laughed.

Emma thanked them and invited them to visit her and the crabs. She hinted, "That would be grand."
As they walked away, Stephen and Shannon looked at each other and noted, "This day has been fun and a little wacky. It's the kind of day that no one would've thought of or planned."

When Emma backed out of the parking lot, inside the box Flam whispered to Sam, "Where are we now? Where do you think she's taking us?"
The hermit crabs were alarmed when they heard a big loud noise coming down the street. It was a school bus!

Flam acted silly and knew better. He giggled, "Sam, Sam, that noise is loud like the ocean. Could that be a big, old whale or an octopus?"
Sam snapped, "Flam, will you calm down? Why must you act so dumb?"

By that time, Emma and the crabs were riding smoothly in the traffic.
Emma was happy and humming until she had to slam on brakes abruptly. Humming changed to panic really quick.

The crabs slid all over the box. They were so terrified that they jerked their large purple claws in front of their shells to close themselves off for safety.
In fear Emma screamed loudly, "My crabs, my crabs!" Things quickly felt crazy and scary.

She pulled the car over to check on the state the crabs were in.
Emma roared in astonishment when she saw that their box was on the floor upside down! She picked up the box to look inside and realized that the crabs were just fine. Emma was relieved and continued to drive again.

There was no way for Emma to have known what had really gone on inside the box. Flam was horrified—like so many times before—
Because Sam had been thrown over harshly. Sam had hit his shell so hard that he lay silently on the floor.

Flam moved over to try and help Sam. He couldn't take much more.
Since Flam was upset, he lamented, "Sam, oh Sam, if we were fish, we wouldn't have ever come onto shore."

By that time, Flam was so upset he gasped for breath, stammered, and cried, "S-S-S-Sam, t-t-tell me you're all right.
Please get up and talk to me. Or are you going to die?"

Sam tried to move. Still dazed, disoriented, and confused, he begged, "Flam, please don't cry.
This hasn't been an easy time. Don't worry. I'll be fine."

The forever friends huddled really close to each other. They feared what might be coming next.
"My, oh my, oh my," wailed Sam, "everything that happens to us is so complex.

Whatever that woman has done, she's put me in a spell. I need a little rest. I'm tired from being tossed about. This crazy activity has nearly cracked my shell."

In shock Flam replied, "Oh, I'm really petrified. Let's get out of here."
Sam felt exhausted and complained, "Flam, you're really getting on my nerves. Be quiet so we can hear."

Finally Emma drove into her garage and turned off the ignition. She rushed to the back of her car and hoped there wouldn't be a problem since she'd left the box of crabs on the floorboard.
Urgently Emma picked up the box to look inside. Surprisingly the crabs looked fine. Emma began loudly clamoring, "We made it. We're home. I got us home and I've been frightened to the core!"

After all of that, Emma walked excitedly into her house with the box of crabs in her hand. She set them on the table close to the door.
She looked out the window and saw that it was raining. "Wow," she exclaimed, "we beat the rain. What a downpour!"

FEELS LIKE THE BEACH AGAIN

Emma wasted no time getting everything in place. She felt tired and tuckered out, and she knew the crabs were too. She opened their box to check on them. She spoke to them from her heart, "My little friends, I know it's been a very long day. You've been without a proper living environment for way too long. But things have changed. Everything is going to be okay."

Without hesitation, Emma carried the crabs into a room. She set them beside where the crab tank sat on a long table. She'd purchased one small dish for their food. She had two large, heavier, shallow saucers for their waters. Since mold can become a problem, the water saucers had to be heavy enough not to turn over as the crabs would play.

Emma proceeded to put objects into the *crabitat*, the pet name for a tank. One heavy saucer held marine salt water. The other held non-chloride water. When crabs submerge into the waters, they hydrate their shells, drink the waters, and soak in them. To survive, crabs need both waters. The waters should be deep, because healthy hermit crabs won't drown.

Putting pebbles, marbles, or rocks into their water saucers gives crabs traction so they can safely get in and out. Once they've left the ocean, instead of lungs, hermit crabs have modified gills that help them breathe underwater. They can also breathe water from the air. When given their essential needs, crabs can live from 10 to 30 years. They just need a safe, healthful environment where they'll have fun. This is their happy hermit-crab playground.

The six-inch moist substrate that Emma had on the floor of the crabitat gave enough depth for hermit crabs to dig a cave for molting, sleeping, and having great places for hiding.

She had decorated the tank with many crab necessities from the list she'd made using the research she'd done about crabs, especially from research on apparatus materials for climbing.

Emma continued to be busy. Meanwhile inside the crabs' box, Sam heard sniffles from Flam. Being concerned, Sam asked, "Flam, what's wrong? Are you crying?" Flam whimpered, "Yeah, I'm crying a little. Sam, I'm disappointed. I thought after that woman took us from the cage in the Superstore at the beach, things would change for us really fast."

Sam moved his body outward from his shell to touch Flam lovingly and comfort him as he responded, "Flam, I feel almost the same. It's confusing. But don't worry. I believe better happenings will take place. Those will surprise both of us, I guess. Then we'll be happy at last."

Emma had placed their crabitat close to a window. She thought the natural sun rays the crabs would receive would be the best during the daytime. There was a stand-up reading lamp for extra lighting beside the overstuffed chair where Emma could sit and watch the crabs move and play anytime.
If crabs have too much light, they become inactive and unhappy. That's the *last* thing Emma wanted for her crabs, so she worked gladly on all the changes. It would be a tragedy if her crabs weren't happy. Hermit crabs are nocturnal creatures and become very active at nighttime. They move around and play a lot. And they eat most of their foods at night.

Therefore, it's best to put their fresh fruits, vegetables, and proteins in the crabitat after sundown. The crabs will go to the food and dig right in. Each crab uses its small right claw primarily to eat. A crab also uses that claw to grab small objects and to scoop up water to drink. To see crabs lift foods to their mouths is adorable and neat. Crabs eat slowly and take small bites.
Emma placed a hamster saucer in their crabitat, because hermit crabs have fun walking around and around in it until daylight.

Emma thought about sitting in her chair and being entertained by watching the crabs until she became sleepy with droopy eyes.

Humidity and warmth are two critical essentials that crabs must have to survive.
Emma analyzed everything she'd done in order for them to stay alive.

Moisture in the tank needs to stay at 70 to 80 percent for the crabs to thrive. Suffocation is the biggest reason they die.
Green moss is pretty in a habitat and creates dampness that they must have to exist. Hermit crabs would be happy and satisfied with a pile of moss to munch on. Moss gives them another place to burrow under, to explore, and in which to hide.

Hermit crabs can't make warmth with their bodies. Emma had attached a warming pad to the side of the tank. If the pad had been placed on the bottom of the tank, it could have produced too much heat for them to play, dig, burrow (which is what they love to do), molt, and sleep.
Emma talked out loud to herself, "I'm ready for my crabs to be in their crabitat having fun. It's decorated enough. I hope the crabs will think it's their paradise. I've worked really hard getting it all together, but it was enjoyable labor. I'd have to say I feel that it is sweetly complete."

Emma already knew she'd want to buy more hermit crabs
   to have an abundantly larger family. Finally the time
   had come for her to pick up the crab box and open it.
By then, Sam and Flam acted sad, confused, and
   eerily quiet.

Suddenly Emma's great big hand grabbed Sam up like a
   spear.
Then her hand set him down inside this new place as
   though he were a souvenir.

After that, in went Flam on top of Sam. The two of them
   were stacked.
You couldn't help but laugh at them as they rode
   piggyback.

Flam's eyes bulged out as he yelped, "Sam, what is this?
   Where are we? Where could we be?"
Sam retorted, "Flam, how would I know? It's too dark and
   black to see!"

After both of them became aggravated and fussed, they
   heard the flick of a switch. Then they saw a light.
In no time at all, it got so warm inside that they thought
   the light was sunshine.

Flam breathed deeply. "Gosh, that's the best I've felt for a
   while. I've been so cold," he chimed.
The hermit crabs felt as though they were back at the
   beach again. It gave them such delight!

Sam and Flam had been placed in a great new home.
A glass tank with lots of space, a securely-fitted lid, humidity, warmth, and plenty of room for them to roam.

Boy, their new home was s-o-o-o-o-o-o-o-o-o good and felt much like what they had known.
The two friends climbed up and down on flowerpots, half logs, and bridges to explore. Then they climbed up and down on piles of stones.

Getting attention is something hermit crabs really adore. Digging caves, hiding anywhere, and burrowing under branches are good pastimes that put the crabs into a wonderful mood.
As they do all those things, you might hear them make chirping sounds. They communicate the way all hermit crabs should.

The crabs moved around in their adventurous crabitat with a jungle of nets, rocks, pieces of rope, and vines with different-sized shells as well as some driftwood too. Climbing here and there is the way hermit crabs behave. In the wild, they're known to ascend all over trees.
Understand that whatever they climb on is considered a plaything that they need.

Lots and lots of toys for play were in their tank. Toys such as Ping-Pong™ balls that are perfect and Barbie®-size basketballs. I guess you can't beat that!
Hermit crabs push those balls all around the tank, investigate them, and topple over them. Those are

all great fun. What a time Sam and Flam had playing in their new crabitat!

The day was coming to an end. It was time for Emma to rest. She grabbed a cup of coffee and settled into her comfortable chair. As she looked inside the crabitat and admired how good it appeared, she saw some movement from the crabs. Emma felt so proud of all she'd done that she couldn't pretend.
She began to tell the hermit crabs her feelings about having been lucky to have found them that day. "I feel sure that we are going to be forever friends."

When Flam heard that statement, he could've lost his shell right then and there. He became so upset that he blurted out, "Sam, did you hear what she said? That's what *we* agreed to be. That's just for *you and me.*" "Yes, I heard her, Flam," stated Sam. "I wish you would calm down.
Remember: she's given us a great new home, so what are you expecting now?

What would be wrong with being grateful and having the three of us be a pack?"
Flam blurted out once again, "Oh no, she's made me mad!" He began to throw a tantrum by hitting his large, purple, hard-as-a-rock claw against the floor. Then he went into a corner to pout. *"We're* the forever friends, not her," he murmured. He kept murmuring to himself until he was worn-out. Almost asleep, Flam complained, "She put a gap in my plans. What an attack!"

By that time, outside the crabitat, Emma was lightly snoring. Because the snoring woke her, she snickered at herself. When she realized what had taken place since she'd fallen asleep while she enjoyed watching the crabs and sleepily tried to get herself up to go to bed, that's when she snickered again.

THE NEIGHBOR KIDS MEET SAM AND FLAM

By early morning, Emma was at the market to get fresh foods and fruits for her crabs. After returning home, she called her neighbor Lynn and asked her to send Ricky and Cindy over after school. Emma told Lynn, "I bought their favorite cookies at the market. I also have a big surprise waiting for them then."

It wasn't long before Ricky and Cindy knocked on her door. They were beside themselves and so excited that they repeated her name over and over, "Ms. Emma, Ms. Emma, we're here!" Each of them gave her a big grin.

As they came in, Emma greeted the children and told them, "The cookies and milk are on the table as usual. They're ready for you to dig in." They ate their snacks faster than she'd ever seen. Not one minute did they linger.

The children's anticipation was obvious as they anxiously waited to hear her big surprise. *What could it be?* They couldn't imagine. Emma took them into the room where the crab tank sat and opened it. She lifted one crab out by its shell and carefully placed it on the floor. She told them to keep an eye on the crab because it can easily disappear. Ricky and Cindy reacted with amazement. Their faces were aglow, and their mouths and eyes were wide open in awe of what they saw. The two hollered excitedly, "Hey, we've seen those before at the Superstore." Ricky asked, "May I hold it?" Emma answered seriously, "Yes, if you want that crab to clamp onto your finger."

Both children backed away and squealed, "No, no, I'm afraid!" Emma added, "It pays to be afraid, because the end of each crab claw is needle sharp. I'm sure you noticed that I picked up the crab by its shell as you must always do. So that it could crawl, I set it on the floor instead of placing it somewhere higher. Those higher places can be really dangerous. If the crab falls, it could hurt itself."

Curiously Ricky asked, "Would it die?" Solemnly Emma responded, "Most likely. A hermit crab can seldom live after having fallen hard from a high place." As the crab moved around and over a toy Emma had put down, the children became quiet, watched closely, and listened to all that Emma said. Suddenly Cindy spoke, "I want a crab like that for myself!"

With concern, Emma questioned, "Cindy, do you know enough about hermit crabs to have one or more as a pet or pets?" "No, I don't. But I know you'll teach me, Ms. Emma," was Cindy's answer. Emma was so touched by that reply that she declared to Cindy, "I'm going to tell you two a story about buying crabs. Here we go! Hermit crabs are sold at most stores at any beach for a small price.

They're put into small plastic containers used for carrying them home only. However, their owners keep the crabs in those containers to entertain their children. They don't realize that crabs have special needs in order to survive. Their crabs usually die. Because of that, hermit crabs become throwaway pets." At the end of the story, Ricky and Cindy sat there speechless and sad. Cindy began to weep with tears rolling down her cheeks. She lamented, "That story made me cry." Ricky agreed. Emma pulled the children close with a hug and dried the tears from Cindy's eyes.

After the hug, Ricky and Cindy looked around and spotted the crab climbing on Emma's drape! Emma gasped, went to pick him up, and put him back in the tank. By then, the crab needed humidity anyway. Emma told the children that crabs are living in a whole new world after having been taken into captivity from the wild. "Do either of you have any questions about crabs' lifestyle?" Ricky asked the first question, "What do they eat?" Emma stated, "Ricky, crabs eat almost anything because they're *scavengers.*

However, when they eat a proper diet, that makes them healthier."

Emma picked up her list of crab foods. "Let's just see what they eat. How about kale, romaine lettuce, spinach, and carrots for a start?" "Wow," Ricky declared. "Crabs really like vegetables. Do they like everything?" "Not really," was Emma's answer, "but they eat quite a variety." Ricky wasn't satisfied yet and asked, "Do they like beets?"
Emma snickered a little over the child's strange question about beets.

Ricky continued, "I like beets because they're red. Not spinach. It's green. I do like green lettuce and broccoli though." Emma really snickered then. She voiced, "Here are some protein and other choices for crab foods: chicken, eggs, nuts, olive oil, and all raw meats." Ricky spoke with deep concentration, "I like chicken thighs."
Emma was getting a kick out of this conversation. "Okay," she said, "let's look at fruits on the list. That will be fun. Apples, grapes, bananas, chopped fruits, and mangoes." Though Cindy was on the quiet side, she finally uttered, "Boy, crabs eat a lot of foods. Some that I don't like." Emma queried the girl, "What would those be?" "I don't like carrots, oooh, or mangoes," Cindy listed. "But I like pies!"

As she *really* laughed, Emma stated, "Pies are not on the crab-foods list." "I know," Cindy agreed. "I just thought of pies. I think crabs would like them. They're good." Then Emma mentioned, "I bet I know one thing both of you like that crabs like too." The children didn't know what to say except, "Ms. Emma, hurry and tell us!" Loudly she announced,

"Peanut butter!" They hollered, "Yeah," with surprise. It was time to steer their minds in another direction, so Emma said, "Let's discuss hermit-crab shells. Do you want to?" Cindy was really excited and declared, "Oh boy, I love pretty shells." Emma began to teach and describe proper crab shells. First she explained that not all shells are the best for hermit crabs. Emma elaborated, "Crabs need specific types of shells. Instead of narrow ones, round shells are the best. Each shell needs to have a wide opening in the shape of the letter *D* or round like the letter *O*. It's best if the shell is light in weight." Then she continued with, "Never buy painted shells. Although they're pretty, the paints are toxic for crabs. The best type of shell is a turbo shell that reminds you of a turban you'd wear on your head. Since a shell isn't a part of the crab's body, the crab must find a borrowed one that perfectly fits its size."

~~~

Finally Emma told Ricky and Cindy, "That's enough information for today. Hey, I'm going to let you two in on a little secret." Their eyes sparkled as they looked up at her with anticipation and eagerly bellowed, "Tell us, tell us, Ms. Emma." Emma leaned down and softly whispered with animation, "In a couple of weeks, I'm going to the Superstore to buy some more hermit crabs. What do you think about that?" With exhilaration the children jumped up and down, "May we go? May we go with you to the Superstore?" "Well, we'll talk about that later," responded Emma. They all said good-bye, and the children left. Inside the tank, Sam and Flam had enjoyed all of Emma's activities with the children and everything they'd heard her teach them about hermit crabs.

Emma took the fresh food she'd bought from the refrigerator. She placed it in the crabs' small dish for eating and to keep their crabitat clean until she removed the leftovers in the morning. Emma looked at herself in the mirror. She looked tired and drab.

She thought, *What a wonderful day this has been. It has ended. And I'm glad, because I have no energy left.* She yawned as she reached for the overhead-light switch and called, "Good night, my little friends!"

As Emma walked away, Flam spoke up thoughtfully, "Sam, you know the children called our owner Ms. Emma. And you're right. She's really nice. Let's call her Ms. Emma like the children did." Happily Sam spoke, "Flam, I'm proud of you because now we're thinking alike."

The forever friends touched their claws together in perfect harmony.

TWO NEW FRIENDS AND A SHELL

Well, it was just the two of them until a certain day
When their owner, Ms. Emma, put a batch of hermit crabs
   into where they played.

Little ones and big ones all got in Flam's way.
He complained, "Who set this up? I won't let them stay!"

Sam suggested, "Come on, Flam. Let's play some games!
Once we get acquainted, they won't seem so strange."

Flam began to check out the other hermit crabs with a
   resentful attitude.
He was annoyed and even picked some fights. Flam was
   very rude.

He wouldn't allow the little ones to play as they could.
Flam stayed in their way and refused to move. He challenged them, "I won't let you through."

The little ones had no choice, so they burrowed into the sand and dirt.
The other hermit crabs never wanted to fight with Flam. They were afraid that they would get hurt.

After a while Flam settled down, fell asleep, and rested well.
Suddenly a noise startled him, and he blared, "Someone fell!"

He heard a voice murmur, "I'm Sue. Sorry I woke you. Someone pushed me as I climbed. So how do you do?"

Flam became nervous and started stuttering, "Awww shucks, it's…it's…it's OK. I…I was just…just taking a nap.
My…My name is Flam. Would you…Would you like to play?"

Flam and Sue climbed up and down on the wood and rocks and had so much fun.
Out of the blue, the hermit crabs in the sand and dirt squealed, "Look what Lulu's done!"

As Sue heard her best friend's name, she quickly looked up.

When Sue turned away from Flam, he just stood there looking stunned.

All the other hermit crabs were hollering, "Lulu lost her shirt!"
"No, no, no," one crab yelled. "Her *shell*. Not her shirt."

As Lulu climbed cautiously, carefully, and slowly toward the light, Flam thought he would die.
There she was without a shell. What a naked sight!

All the hermit crabs scrutinized Lulu's progress intently, with their antennas flying high.
Sam implored, "Don't hurt her. You know you must be kind.

Move on over. Give Lulu plenty of space as she tries to find
A brand-new shell that fits her size. She's already left her shell behind."

Flam fretted and fumed, "I don't care. She can't do that. Lulu's taking up our time!"
Sam grabbed Flam firmly with his large, purple claw and commanded, "Don't move an inch. You're being terribly unkind!

You know what Lulu must do in order to survive.
She has to find the perfect shell soon, or else she just might die."

All at once without warning, it was quiet. You couldn't hear a sound.
Every hermit crab was frozen in its place as Lulu moved around.

It didn't take long until the little hermit crab seemed to be in a spell as she flipped into the perfect-sized shell.
She was like an actress on a stage who knows her part really well.

Then Lulu sang proudly to all the other hermit crabs from her new shell, "I'm growing big like you."
Sam teased his friend, "Flam, you must admit that Lulu's really cute."

Flam was embarrassed and replied, "Awww, I don't know, Sam. I guess that she'll do."
Sam laughed at his friend and teased, "Are you flirting with her, Flam? You know we all love you."

LITTLE JOHN

Later there was another little hermit crab running all
  around.
The hermit crabs named him Little John. His shell was
  white and brown.

Since he moved faster than the others, he stole their food
  from them.
That left him only one thing to do: *run* in case they
  grabbed.

One fateful day their owner thought she'd pick Little John
  up to play.
She talked gently to him and cooed, "You're sweet," and
  lifted him to her face.

That scared Little John. He was o-v-e-r-w-h-e-l-m-e-d!
He grabbed her chin with his biggest claw and held her like a shell.

Sam gasped, "Oh, look at Little John. He's pinched Ms. Emma's chin!
Oh no, he's grabbed her on her lip. Ow, he'll surely tear her skin."

Every hermit crab witnessed their owner holler loudly. Sam wailed desperately, "Oh, what now?"
He closed his eyes as if to pray. He was afraid to look around.

When their owner managed to get Little John's claw off her lip, she was really mad.
She threw the little hermit crab all the way across the room, acting oh so bad.

Immediately she ran to him. She carefully and gently picked up Little John. The crab didn't act just right.
The owner thought her heart would break and sobbed, "What if my baby dies?"

She gently set poor, pitiful Little John back where he had been. The other crabs knew he was hurt.
By that time, all the other hermit crabs were terrified. Not one said a word.

They wanted Little John to be all right. But they knew he wasn't. They didn't make a stir.
All of them felt sick deep inside because of what had just occurred.

Poor Little John became very quiet. He was afraid that he might die.
He thought sadly, *I've been hurt too badly to pull through and survive.*

It wasn't long before he knew that he had to give up his shell.
The other hermit crabs knew it too. They knew it oh so well.

When Emma noticed the strange movements of the crabs, she knew things had really gone wrong. Their antennas were moving quickly back and forth. Emma was upset, feeling guilty, grieving, and thinking that Little John might be gone. Sure enough, Little John had died. He was far too weak to tell the other crabs good-bye.
All the hermit crabs felt such grief over losing their little friend. They cried and cried and cried.

Each crab in the tank pitched in to dig a special place for his burial as they prepared for his funeral. After John was buried, all the hermit crabs threw kisses to the sky.
Then all the crabs sat down on the ground, with Little John heavy on their minds.

Sam was still upset due to their owner's thoughtless and impulsive actions.
He wondered why she'd treated John so roughly. *Why did she have to be so mean?* He questioned her reactions.

When she picked Little John up to play with him that day, what gave her the right
To throw him across the room? After all, John had only done what a hermit crab does and had put up a fight.

Sam remembered and thought about Little John and Ms. Emma's behavior. He wiped the tears off his face.
He lamented, "Poor little fellow. Good-bye, Little John," as he turned and walked away.

FOREVER FRIENDS

Things got back to normal soon after that. The hermit
 crabs stayed close, made clicking sounds, and chirped.
You'd never believe the sounds they make. They sound
 like frogs that burp.

Sam encouraged, "Flam, it's a brand-new day. Let's eat
 and play some games.
We're just a bunch of hermit crabs. There's nothing we
 can change.

You know we all must forget what's happened in the
 recent past
And go on with our lives the best we can. There's lots of
 climbing here for us, so let's have a blast."

Sam continued, "We should look around and be glad we
    have the perfect home.
Let's rest a bit till nighttime comes. Then the two of us
    can start to roam.

Nighttime is when hermit crabs like us really have loads
    of fun.
We like to climb, to eat, and to clean ourselves. We like to
    show our stuff."

Finally that entire bunch of hermit crabs began to laugh,
    instead of being sad.
They were happy to be alive and glad for all they had.

Sam directed, "In your place, hold hands to dance around
With that someone you'll embrace. We'll look like a
    merry-go-round."

That's exactly what they did as all the hermit crabs
    became good friends.
Everyone danced, embraced, and felt happy then. Even
    Flam settled in.

Then Sam spoke seriously, "Flam, I think it's great that
    we're growing old together.
It's always been just you and me holding on to each other.

Do you remember all the adventures we've had and all
    the times when we thought it was the end?
Yes, we've had our disagreements. But forever we are
    friends.

We've had some strange and exciting escapades too. Wouldn't you agree?
I think we've grown up and become more mature, as anyone can see!"

Acting silly, Flam responded, "Yeah, Sam, two big ugly hermit crabs doing the best we can.
But, Sam, I really do believe you're uglier than I am!

Don't hit me, Sam. I'll be good. You know I'm your best friend.
And you love me. Or at least you should. You've always *said* you did.

Sam, Sam, don't do it. Sam, Sam, remember we're friends. We're forever friends!"
Sam chased Flam and hollered, *"Yeah, we're friends, Flam. Yeah, Flam, we're forever friends!"*

Flam ran as fast as he could.

"Okay, Sam. Okay, Sam. Oh no! Sa-a-a- a-a-a-m-m-m, ..."

S-a-a-a-a-a-m-

Gratitude

Steve Graham, a retired teacher and coach. But even better than that, he's my daughter Connie's husband of 48 years. Steve has always been a great son-in-law.

I'll always be thankful for his patience while Connie has spent a lot of time helping with editing, perfecting, and typing my story. My late husband, the Colonel, would state, "Cinderella, Connie is a saint."

Connie made this book a reality with her energies toward me. I was so blessed the day I had her and continue to be blessed that we have each other.

The newlyweds Stephen and Shannon Graham, my grandson and his wife. They brought Connie and me to Paws and Claws Publishing, LLC, via Donna Smith Lawrence who is Shannon's aunt.

Stephen has told me that when he was little, he listened to *everything* I told him. He was fascinated by all the stories from my life. He's convinced that he's going to write my autobiography since I've had such an interesting life and stories that need to be told.

Donna Smith Lawrence who brought Connie and me to Paws and Claws Publishing, LLC. Donna has published three books about her and Susie, their dog that is the inspiration for Susie's Law in North Carolina, through Paws and Claws. Her chapter book called *Susie's Miracle—The Inspiration Behind Susie's Law* was her first book and the first book that Paws and Claws Publishing published. It was made into the feature-length movie *Susie's Hope* about Donna and Susie.

From the beginning, Donna promoted my book or books and me to Lynn Bemer Coble, my editor. She texted Lynn that "this lady has a story to tell." And so, I did!

About the Author

CharLene Seay is many things: an entertainer, a vocalist, a mother, a grandmother, an actress, a songwriter, a floral and home-decor designer, a Christian, a pianist, and a pet owner of two precious cats, just to mention a few of the many pets she's had throughout her life.

CharLene is a native of Knoxville, Tennessee, and the eldest of four. She came from a musical family. All the family sang in church. Her daddy played guitar and CharLene played the piano. Both played by ear!

After a marriage, two daughters whom she taught to sing and to entertain, and a divorce, she turned professional in the music industry.

Her stage name was simply CharLene. She performed in clubs, lounges, and dining rooms. She also performed in shows. Her music genres ranged widely from gospel to country to pop. She was also very comedic and entertained her audiences.

She became so popular as an entertainer that she was nominated for Best Single Performer by the Knoxville Entertainment Awards. She was also a regular on the "Cas Walker Farm and Home Hour" TV Show in Knoxville. It was a local variety show that ran on TV from 1954 to 1971. Cas Walker was a multimillionaire and an icon in the area. That TV show was the show that got ten-year-old Dolly Parton into the limelight.

During her career, she did lots of CharLene shows including "A Tribute to Dolly." In fact, when CharLene started accepting gigs to appear as a Dolly Parton look-alike, she eventually caught the attention of "PM Magazine." The TV show's crew came to her home to film an interview with her. That night, they came to her shows in Knoxville. One show was "CharLene," and the other was her Dolly Parton tribute. The crew filmed both shows. On the episode in which they featured CharLene, they included the interview and her Knoxville shows. That episode went international. As a result, she heard from Dolly Parton herself via a telegraph message stating, "I'm very flattered and complimented." When the two women

finally met, Dolly said, "Oh my goodness, we look alike." CharLene even worked on a Canadian tour as the only look-alike of Dolly Parton. She worked with a look-alike of Kenny Rogers.

From the huge repertoire of songs that she'd sing for an audience, she often wrote and performed her own original songs as well. CharLene's songs were about life, love, and God. *Cash Box* magazine noticed her and invited her to be a featured artist on the Songwriters Night at the Country Music Hall of Fame® Showcase in Nashville, Tennessee. She appeared under her full name CharLene Seay.

In 1982, CharLene performed at the World's Fair in Knoxville at the Holiday Inn–World's Fair Site. There she performed in an open bar area. She played a piano and sang solo. She also worked with a jazz group and with another kind of band.

At the historical Pat O'Brien's® club ('one of the most iconic nightclubs in the United States') in New Orleans—which is a bar and performance hall—CharLene performed. She'd sent her tape to them and got the job because of the tape. The newspaper reporters in Knoxville wrote about her when she landed that gig.

At Pat O'Brien's®, two women played the same song on copper-topped baby grand pianos that faced each other. They called this The Original Dueling Pianos Show. It's a club favorite. The "'dueling pianos' concept evolved from the late 1890s ragtime era, where two pianists would 'duel' for the crowd's attention and tips."

CharLene began to have gigs in Myrtle Beach, South Carolina, in the 1990s. That was when she became acquainted with hermit crabs. She started to purchase crabs, and they became her pets. She thought they were such fascinating creatures that she continued to buy many, many, many more. Every time she bought them, the clerks in the beach stores exclaimed, "Oh my goodness, those are some lucky hermit crabs!" CharLene bought so many crabs that she had to turn a fish aquarium into a *crabarium*. That's where the story of *Sam and Flam—Forever Friends* originated.

Over the course of her professional career, CharLene performed at a wide variety of venues in Ohio, Tennessee, Florida, Louisiana, North Carolina, and South Carolina. She performed at conventions in Tennessee, Illinois, and Texas. She performed on television and radio in Tennessee, Northern Alabama, and Ohio.

CharLene still plays her grand piano during her free time.

She loved being an entertainer.

You can find some of her original songs on YouTube and Spotify by searching "CharLene Seay."

CPSIA information can be obtained
at www.ICGtesting.com
Printed in the USA
BVHW021016180722
642400BV00018B/103